Abington Public Library
Abington, MA 02351

P9-DFY-665

Abington Public Library
Abington, MA 02351

Little Roja Riding Hood

Susan Middleton Elya

illustrated by Susan Guevara

G. P. PUTNAM'S SONS
AN IMPRINT OF PENGUIN GROUP (USA)

G. P. PUTNAM'S SONS
Published by the Penguin Group
Penguin Group (USA) LLC
375 Hudson Street
New York, NY 10014

USA | Canada | UK | Ireland | Australia
New Zealand | India | South Africa | China
penguin.com
A Penguin Random House Company

Text copyright © 2014 by Susan Middleton Elya. Illustrations copyright © 2014 by Susan Guevara.
Penguin supports copyright. Copyright fuels creativity, encourages diverse voices, promotes free speech, and creates a vibrant culture.
Thank you for buying an authorized edition of this book and for complying with copyright laws by not reproducing,
scanning, or distributing any part of it in any form without permission.
You are supporting writers and allowing Penguin to continue to publish books for every reader.

Library of Congress Cataloging-in-Publication Data
Elya, Susan Middleton, 1955–
Little Roja Riding Hood / Susan Middleton Elya ; illustrated by Susan Guevara.
p. cm.
Summary: A rhyming twist on the classic fairy tale in which a little girl saves her grandmother from a wolf. Includes glossary of Spanish words.
[1. Stories in rhyme. 2. Fairy tales. 3. Folklore.] I. Guevara, Susan, ill. II. Title.
PZ8.3.E514Lit 2013
398.2—dc23
[E]
2012022545
Manufactured in China by South China Printing Co. Ltd.
ISBN 978-0-399-24767-5
1 3 5 7 9 10 8 6 4 2

Design by Marikka Tamura. Text set in ITC Usherwood Std.
The art was done with watercolor, ink and gouache.

To Bill, to grandmothers, and to walking through the woods. —S.M.E.

For Elena Sybella Celia Clark Backus y Herrera and her papa, Nicholas. —S.G.

Glossary

Abue (AH bweh) Gran

(la) abuela (ah BWEH lah) grandma

(la) abuelita (ah bweh LEE tah) little grandma

ay (I) oh my

(el) bosque (BOCE keh) forest

caliente (kah LYEHN teh) hot

(la) canasta (kah NAHS tah) basket

(las) capas (KAH pahs) capes

(la) capucha (kah POO chah) hood

caramba (kah RAHM bah) my goodness

(la) casita (kah SEE tah) little house

(los) colores (koe LOE rehs) colors

(los) dientes (DYEHN tehs) teeth

el, los (EHL, LOS) the (masculine singular and plural)

(las) flores (FLOE rehs) flowers

grande (GRAHN deh) big

la, las (LAH, LAHS) the (feminine singular and plural)

Lobo (LOE boe) Wolf

Mamá (mah MAH) Mom

mi (MEE) my

muy (MWEE) very

(la) nieta (NYEH tah) granddaughter

(la) niña (NEE nyah) girl

no problema (NOE proe BLEH mah) no problem

(los) ojos (OE hoce) eyes

(las) orejas (oe REH hahs) ears

(la) razón (rrah SONE) reason

(la) receta (rreh SEH tah) recipe

Roja (RROE hah) Red

(la) ropa (RROE pah) clothing

sí (SEE) yes

(el) sistema (seece TEH mah) system

(la) sopa (SOE pah) soup

(las) telenovelas (teh leh noe VEH lahs) soap operas

(la) tos (TOCE) cough

tu, tus (TOO, TOOCE) your (singular and plural)

valiente (vah LYEHN teh) brave

(la) voz (VOCE) voice

There once was a **niña** who lived near the woods.
She liked to wear colorful **capas** with hoods.

"**Roja**," called Mom from her **telenovelas**,
"go through the woods till you get to **Abuela**'s.

"She has a bad cough, so take her this **sopa**.
It's **muy caliente**. Don't spill on **tu ropa**.

"Be safe in **el bosque**," **Mamá** warned her child.
"Be careful of anything furry or wild."

"*Sí*," said *la niña*, who left with her basket.
Then from a tree came a question. Who asked it?

"Where are you going in your *capa* so red?"
"To see *mi abuela*," Red suspiciously said.

Then a large wolf appeared. "Look at these *flores*.
Surely your grandma would love *los colores*."

"Hmm, since she's sick, some flowers are good."
She set down her basket, her *capa* and hood.

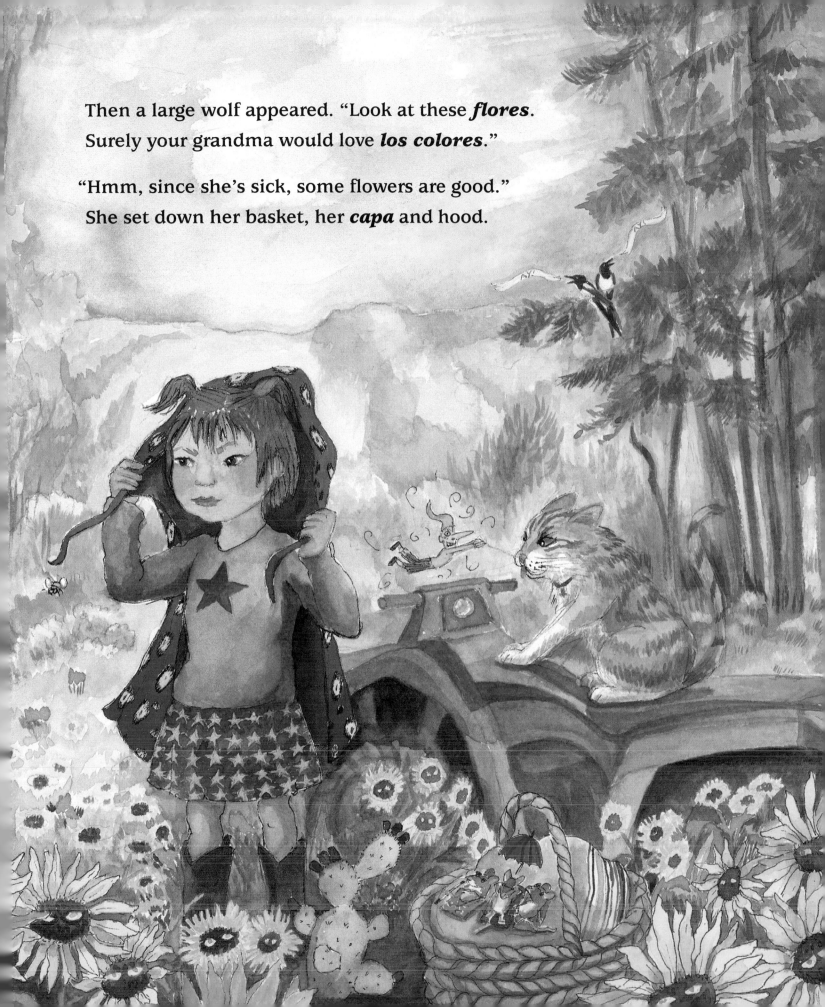

While **Roja** picked blossoms, the wolf sidled off,
complete with disguise, to inspect Grandma's cough.

In cape and **capucha**, he reached **la casita**
and knocked on the door of the sick **abuelita**.

"**Abue**," he said in a high, squeaky **voz**,
"I'm sorry to hear of your terrible **tos**."

"**Roja**, come in! Oh, what a surprise!"
She noticed at once the size of Wolf's eyes.

"**Tus ojos**," she said. "So **grande** the pair!"
"The better to see you!" He sat in her chair.

"**¡Tus orejas!**" she said.
"So furry and dark."
"The better to hear you,"
was Wolf's quick remark.

Then **Roja** walked up with her lovely bouquet.
Somewhere she'd misplaced her **capa** that day.

She peeked in the window and saw her red hood,
and inside it, **Lobo**. **¡Caramba!** Not good!

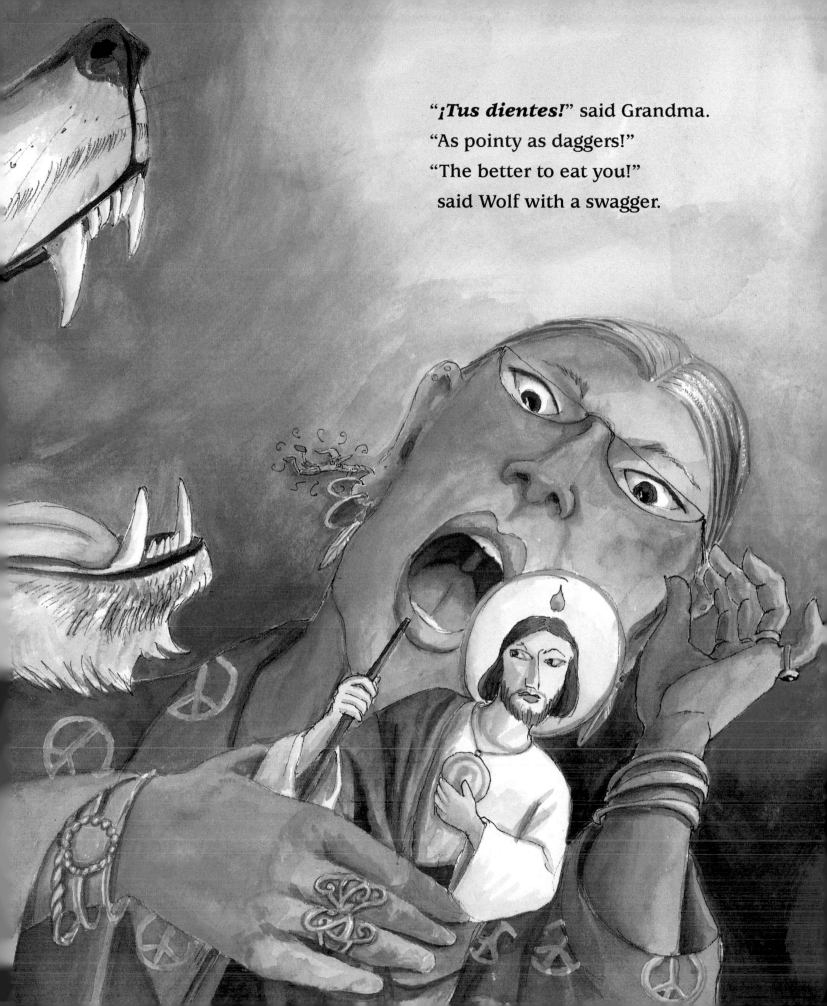

"*¡Tus dientes!*" said Grandma.
"As pointy as daggers!"
"The better to eat you!"
said Wolf with a swagger.

Just then, little **Roja** burst in through the door.
And Grandma? No need to play dumb anymore.

"I won't be your lunch," said Gran. "Phony **nieta**!"
"Some soup, Wolf?" said **Roja**. "My mom's best **receta**!"

She swung **la canasta** and out flew the soup,
too hot for **Lobo**, who soon flew the coop.

"*¡Ay, caliente!*" Wolf said as he ran.

"You saved me!" said Grandma. "But I need a plan."

"To keep yourself safe? Of course. *¡No problema!*"
  They shopped for a lock and security *sistema*.

And now, when folks knock for whatever **razón**,
Abuela's reply is the same, set in stone.

"Just come let me see you!"—and then she'll unlock it.
Of course, Little Red keeps a phone in her pocket.

When traveling through woods,
she's *muy valiente*
and never leaves home
without soup *caliente*!

Abington Public Library
Abington, MA 02351